The Animals

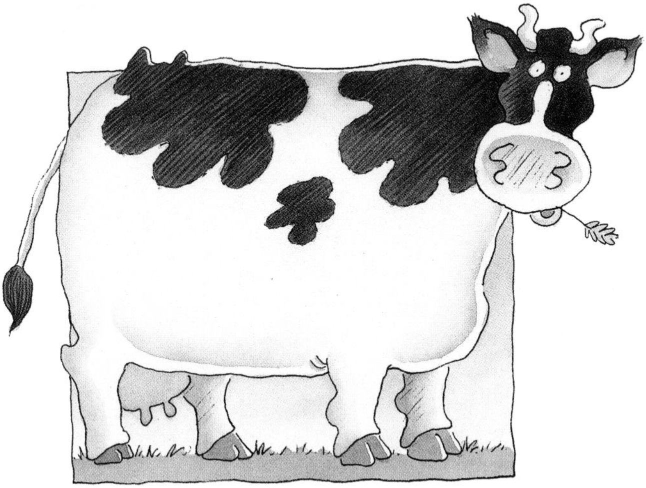

Illustrated by Philip Webb

Rigby

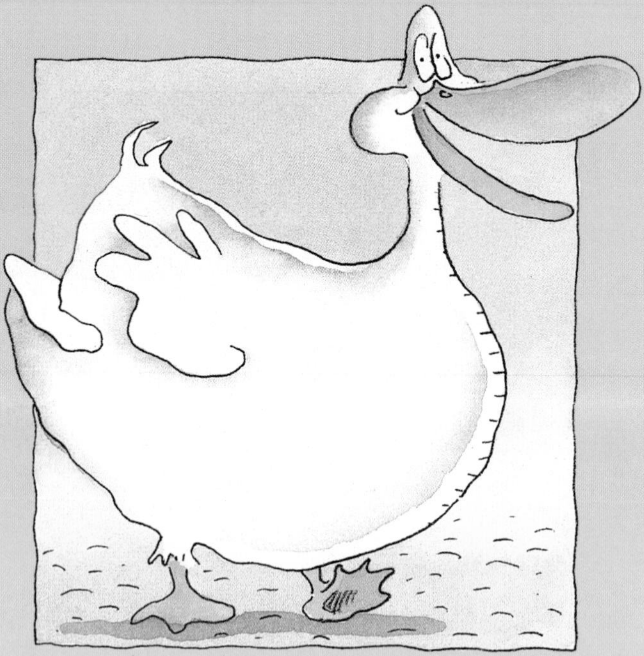

I can quack.

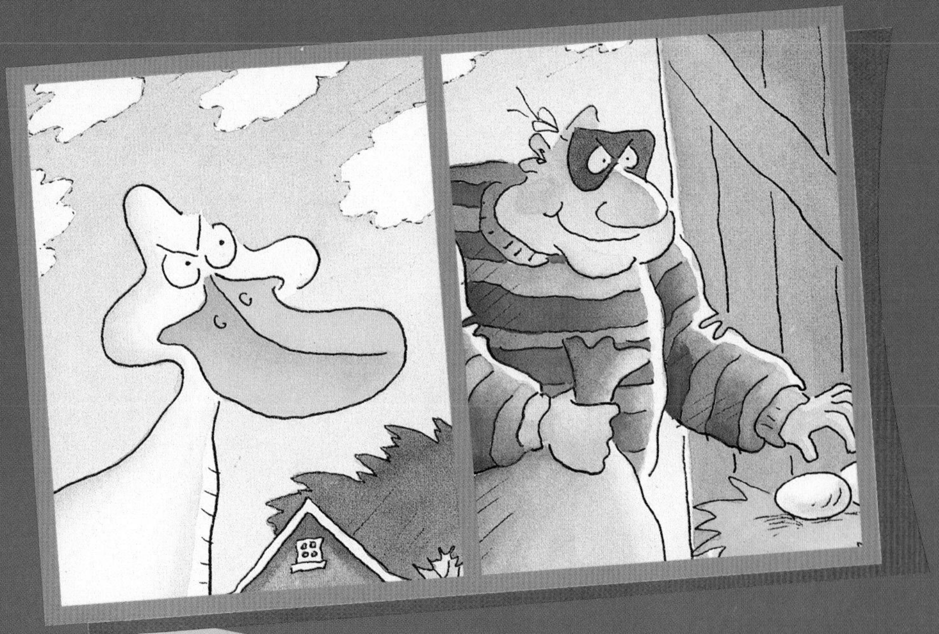

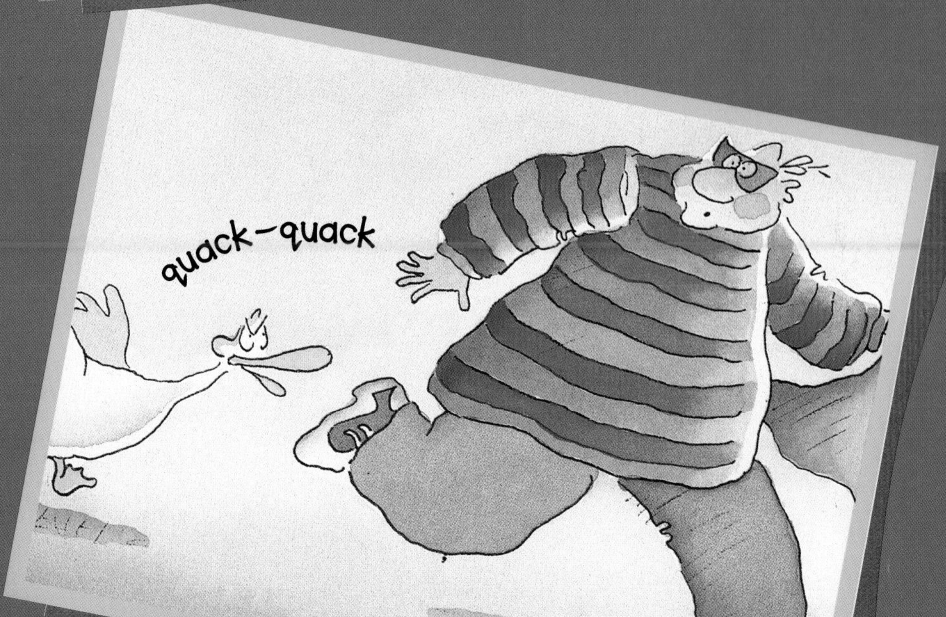
quack-quack

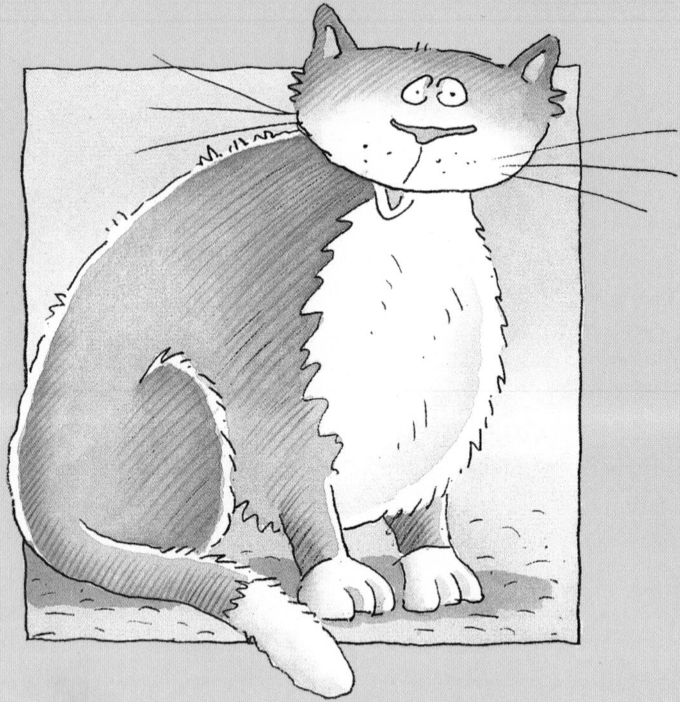

I can meow.

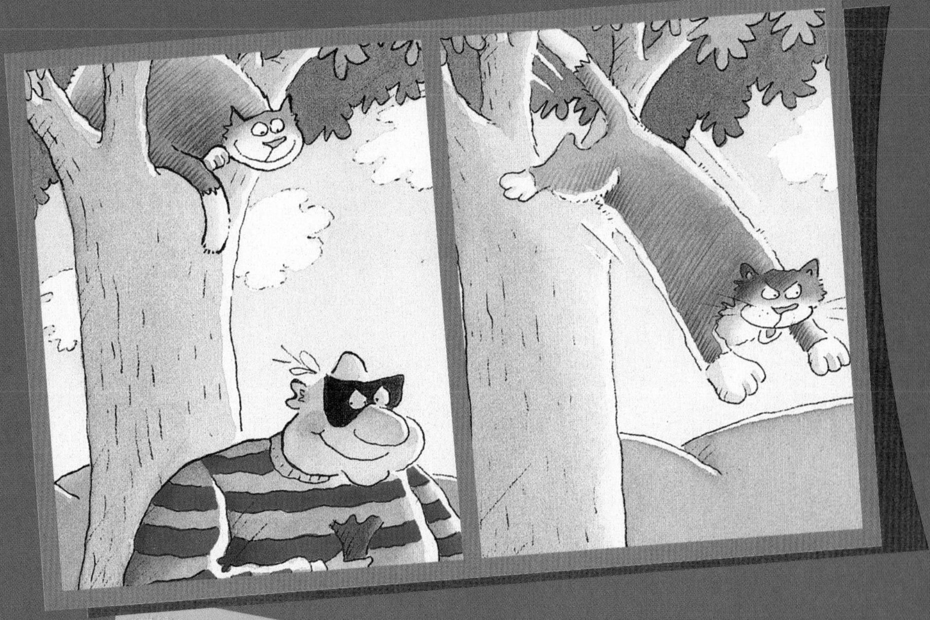

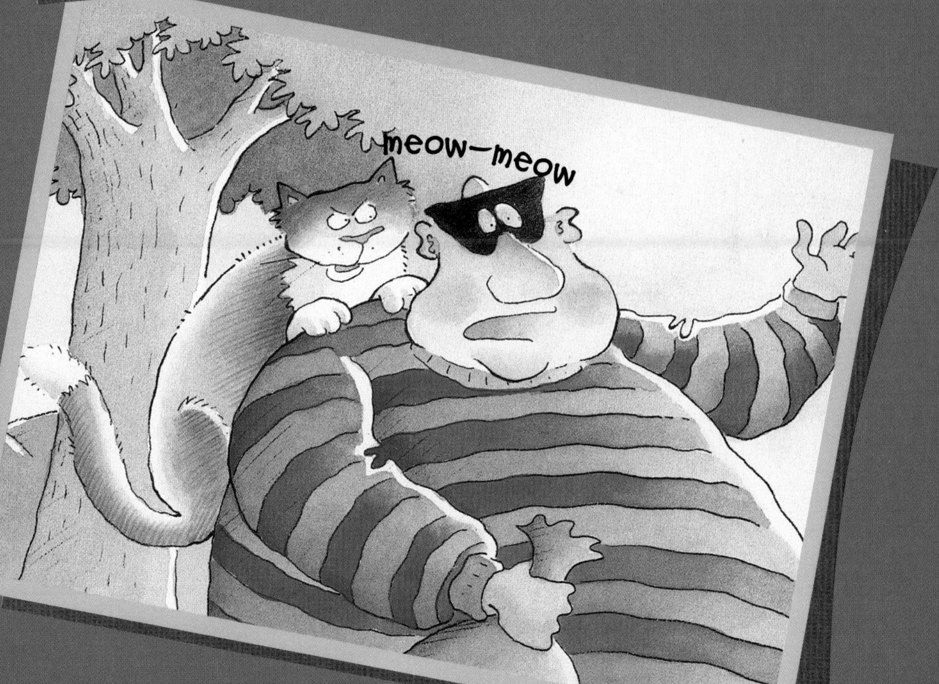
meow–meow

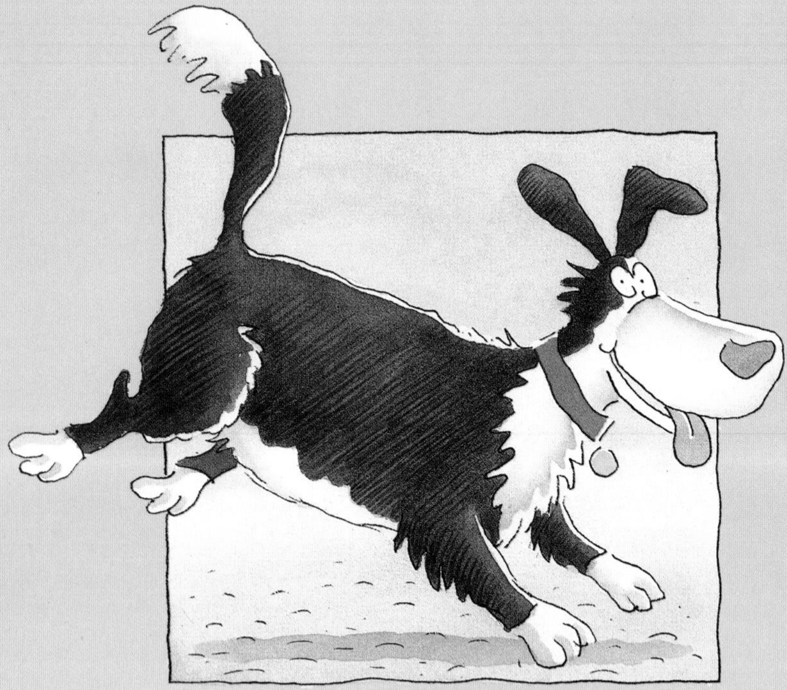

I can bark.

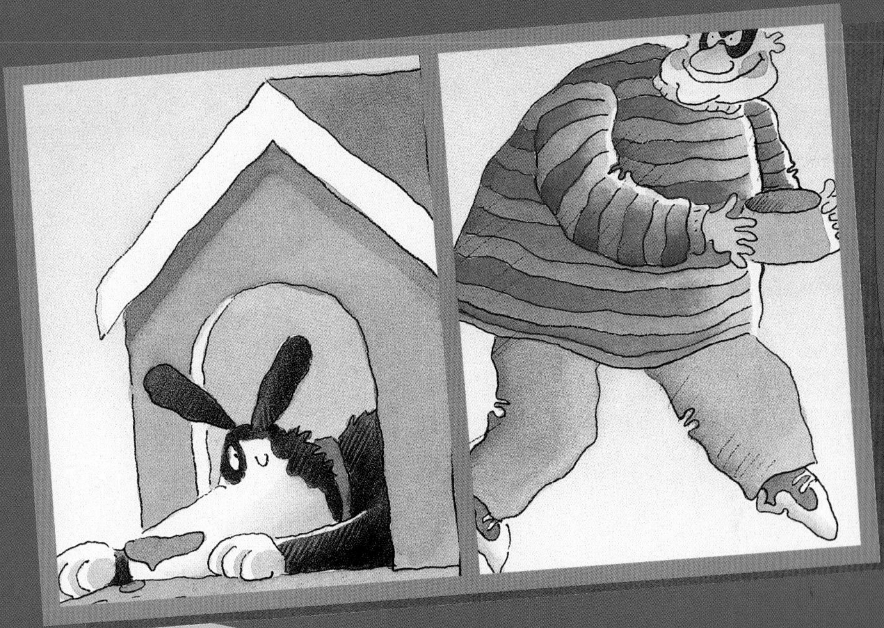

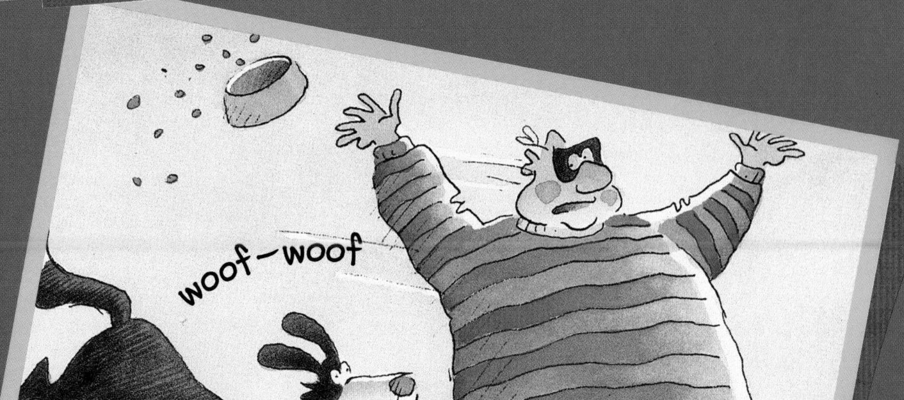
woof–woof

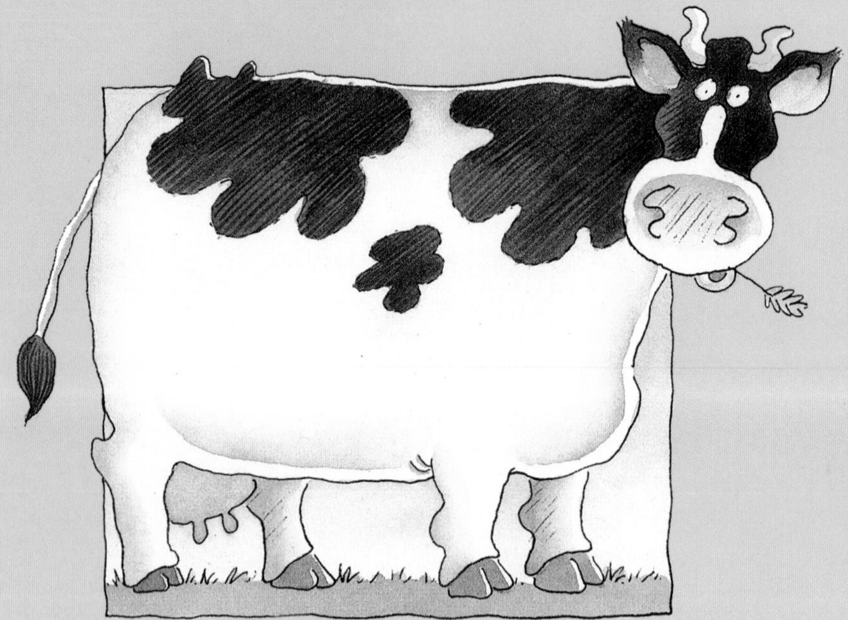

I can moo.

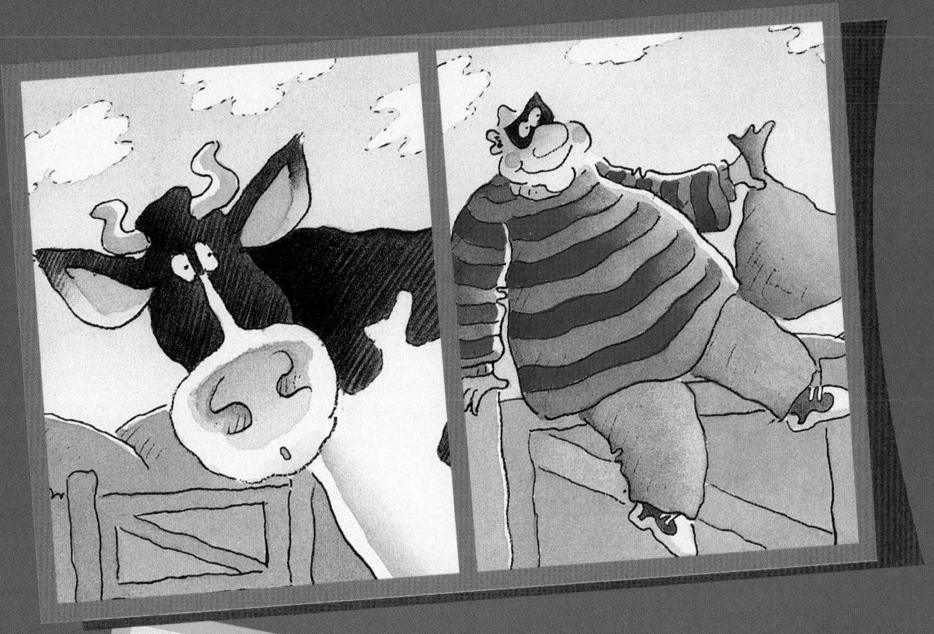

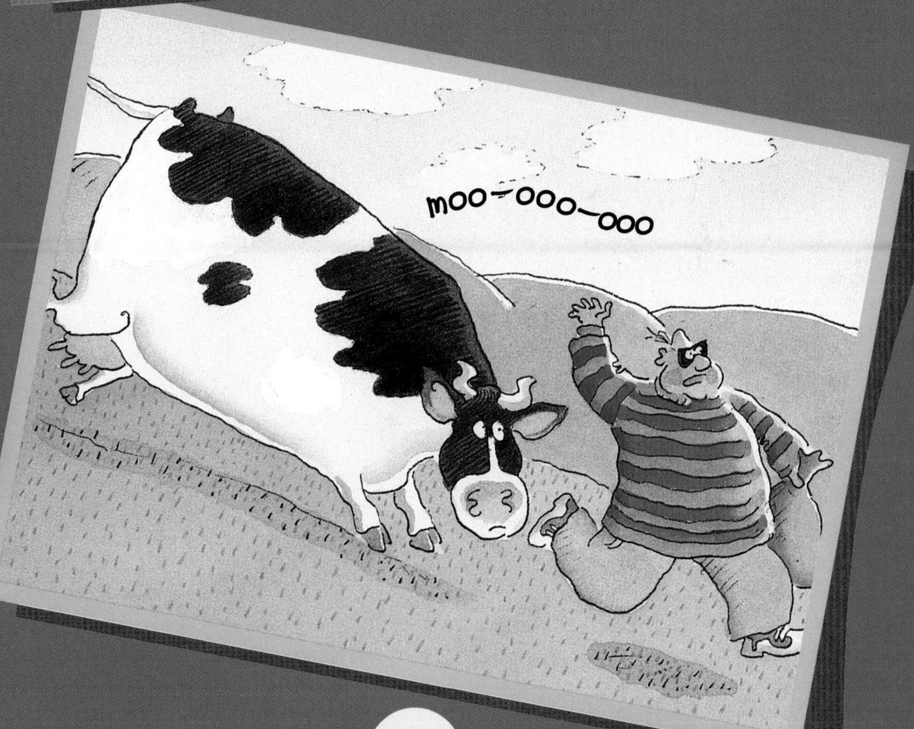
moo-ooo-ooo

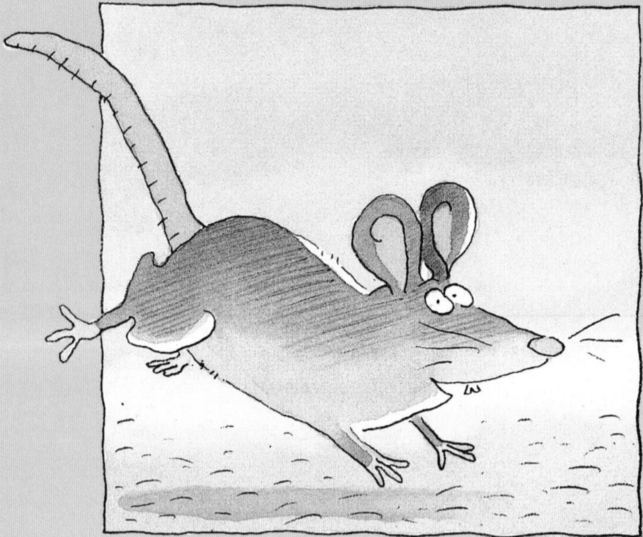

I can squeak.

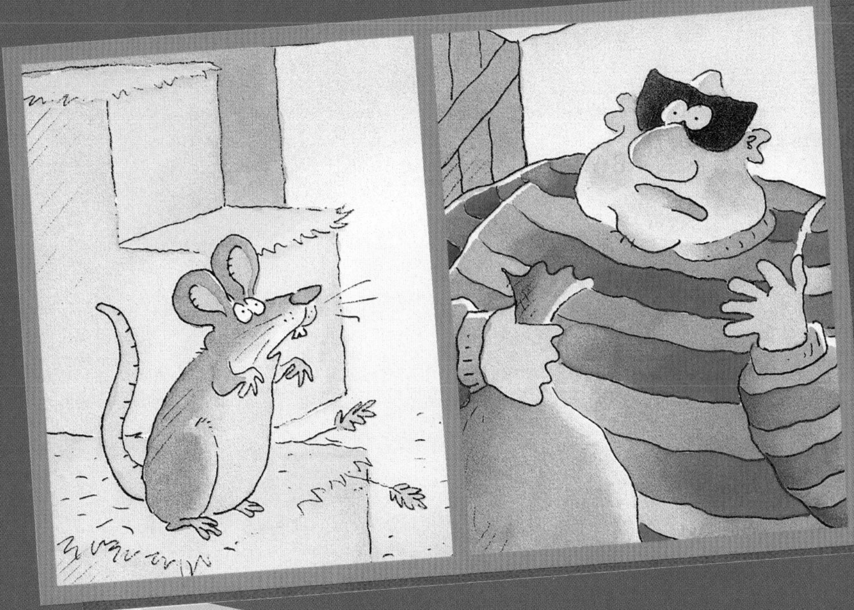

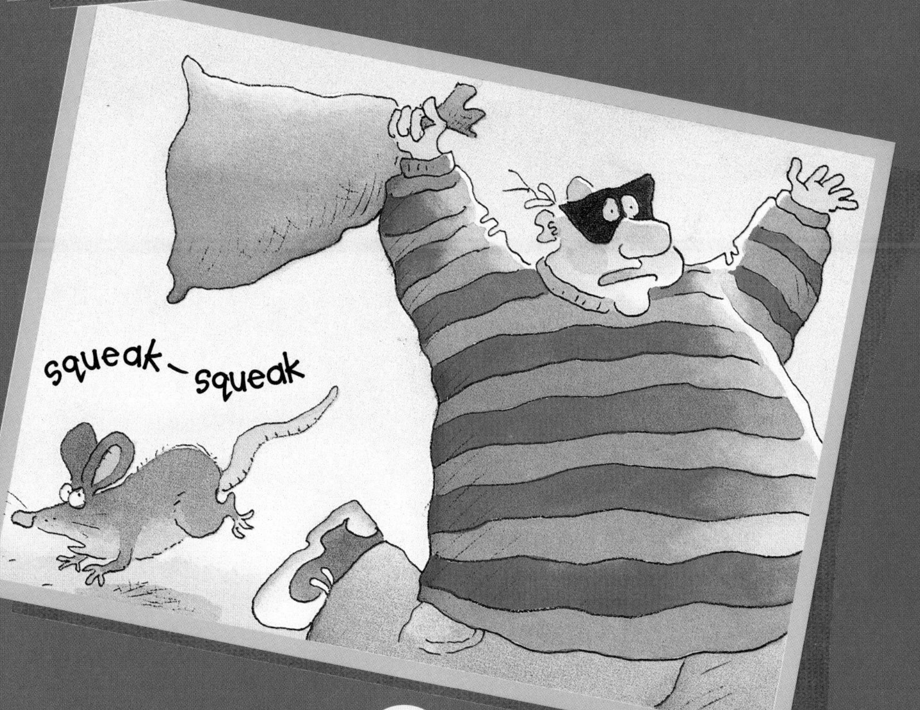
squeak-squeak

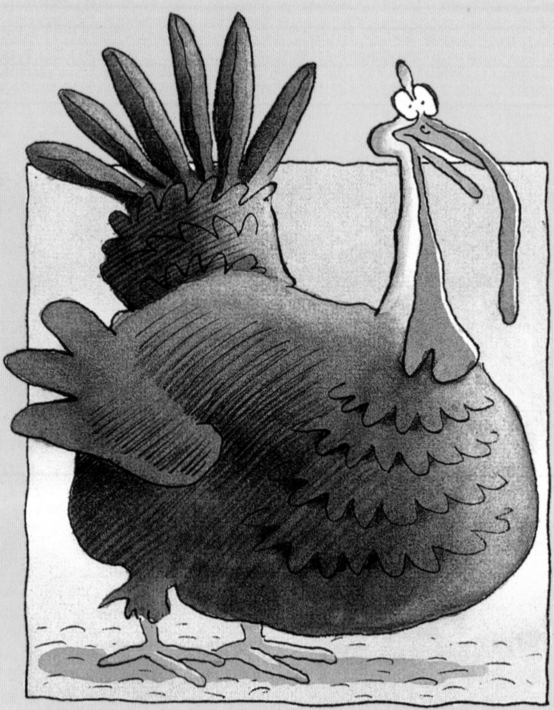

I can gobble.

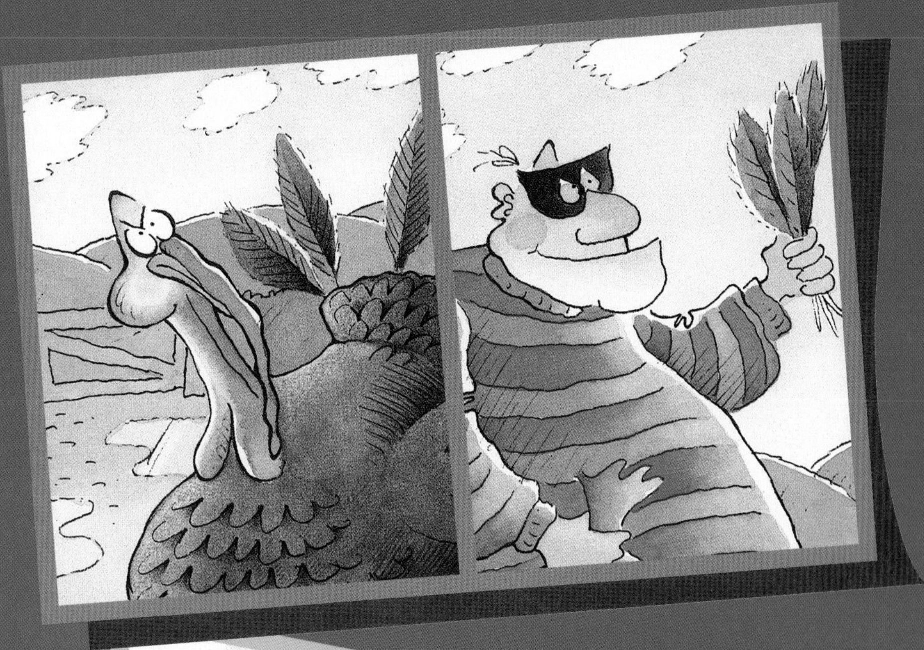

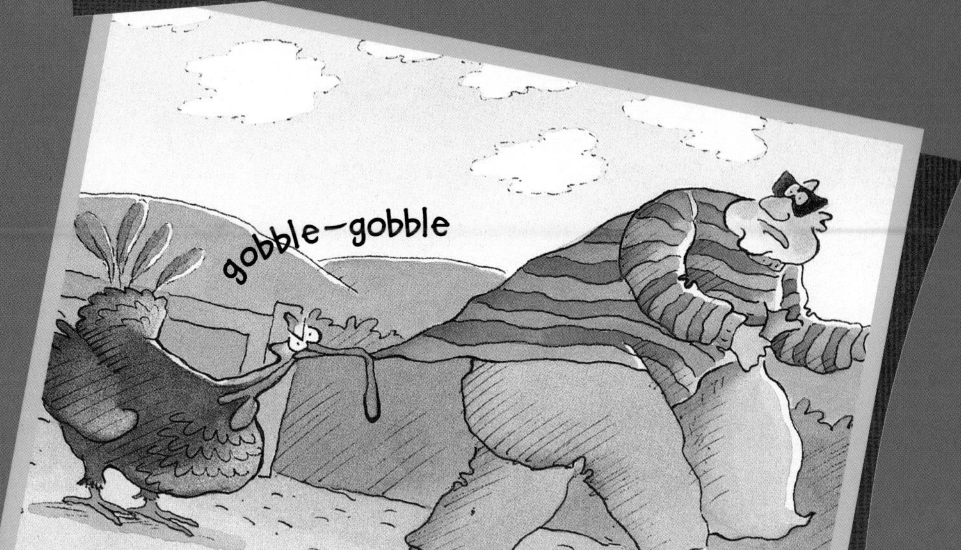
gobble-gobble

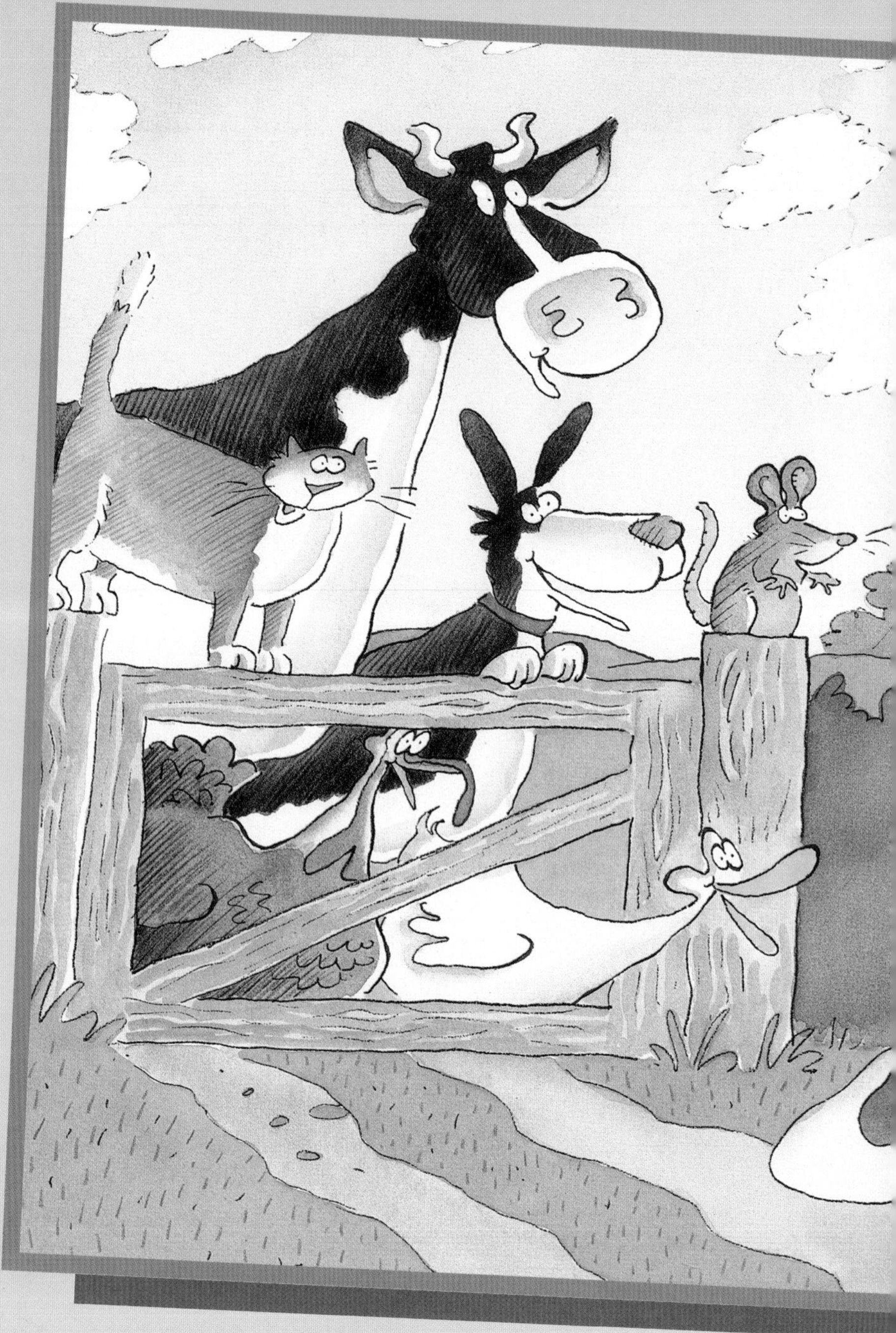

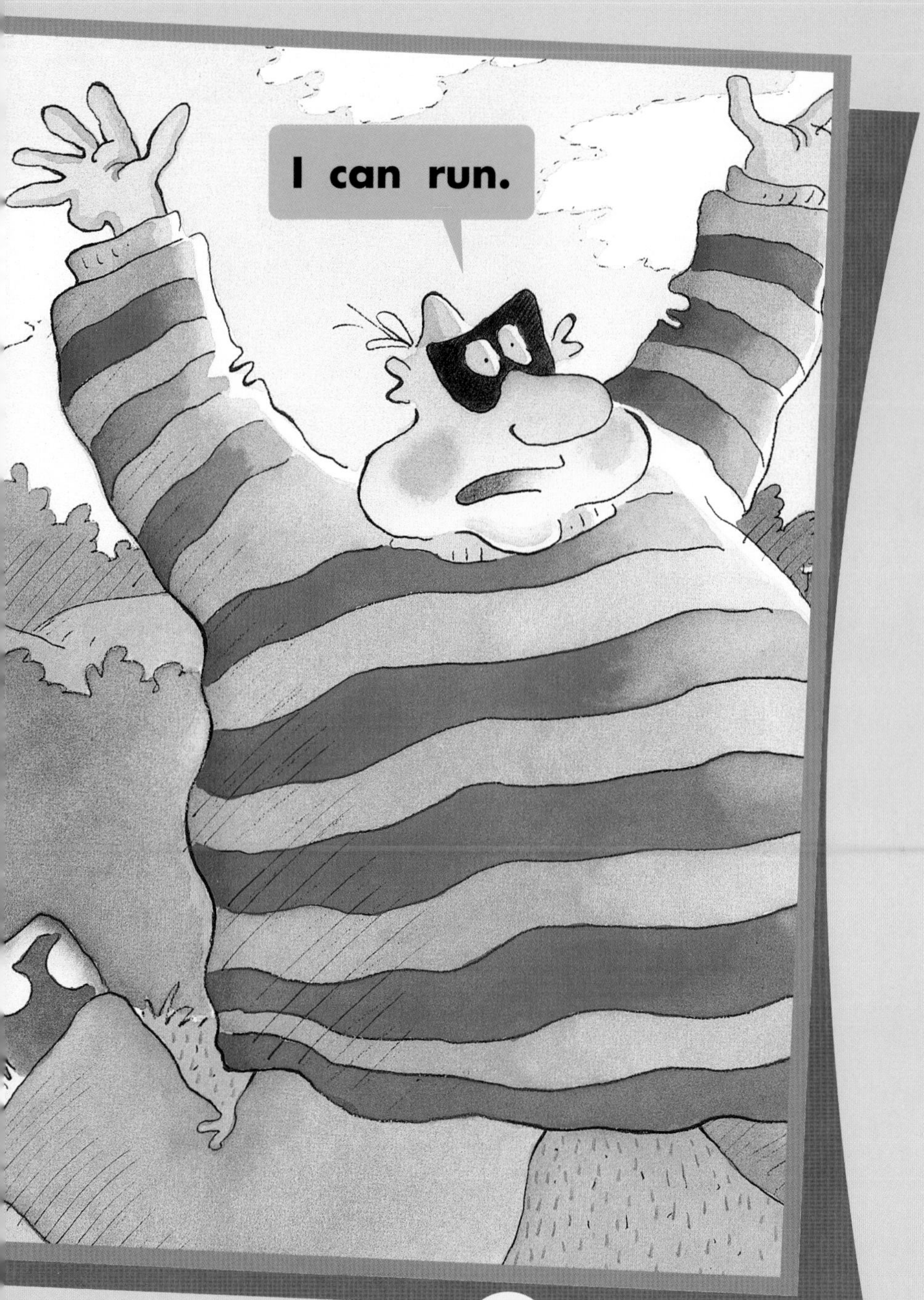
I can run.

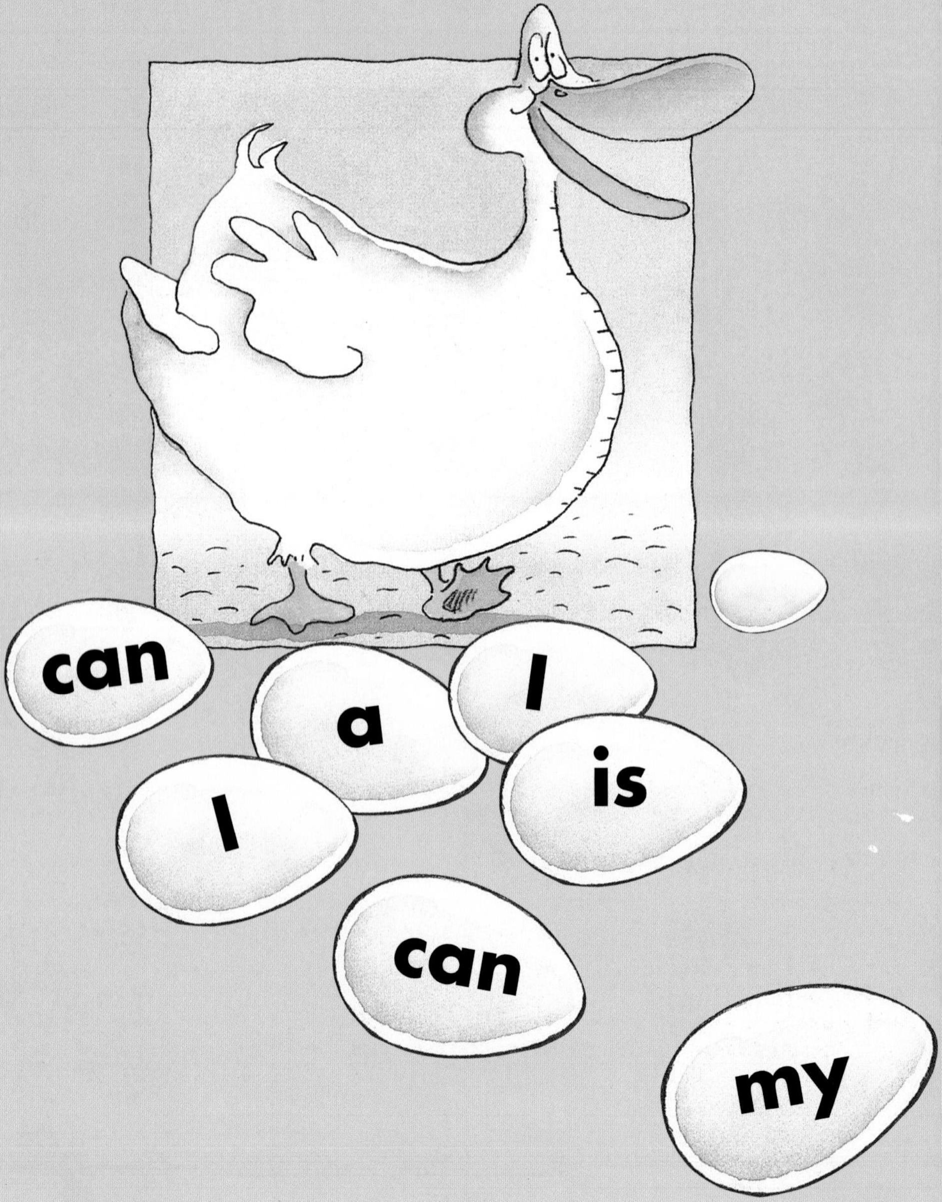
can
a
I
I
is
can
my